GRIND

Dee Phillips

RiGHT NOW!

Blast
Dare
Dumped
Eject
Fight
Friends?

Goal
Goodbye
Grind
Joyride
Mirror
Scout

Property Of
Wisconsin School for the Deaf

First published by Evans Brothers Limited

2A Portman Mansions, Chiltern Street, London W1U 6NR, United Kingdom

Copyright © Ruby Tuesday Books Limited 2009

This edition published under license from Evans Limited

All rights reserved

32000123708762

SADDLEBACK
EDUCATIONAL PUBLISHING
www.sdlback.com

© 2011 by Saddleback Educational Publishing

ISBN-13: 978-1-61651-250-7
ISBN-10: 1-61651-250-4
eBook: 978-1-63078-005-0

Printed in the U.S.A.

20 19 18 17 16   6 7 8 9 10

I didn't want to move to this town.
There's nowhere to skate here.
I miss my friends.
I hate it here.

GRIND

ONE MOMENT CAN CHANGE YOUR LIFE FOREVER

My elbow hurts.
My knees hurt.
It's Saturday afternoon, and
I'm lying outside the library.

My life
couldn't get any
worse!

5

I saw the handrail, and I couldn't resist it.
I thought I could do it.
A nose grind down the handrail.

But I was wrong!

And now I'm lying outside the library.
My new jeans are ripped.

My deck is stuck
in a tree.

I hate this town.
I moved here three weeks ago.
I've been trying to find a place to skate.
But there are NO SKATING signs everywhere.
If I get into trouble, Mom will go crazy!

NO
SKATING
HERE

I moved here three weeks ago with Mom.
Mom is getting married to Paul.
I want Mom and Paul to be happy.
But I hate it here.

Kelsey

Jack

Ellie

I miss my friends.

I miss my friends.
I miss SKATE CITY.
I went to SKATE CITY
all the time with my friends.

There's nowhere to skate here.
There's no skate park.

SKATE CITY

There's something else, too.
Paul has a son.
I will have a new stepbrother called Ethan.
Ethan is older than me. He's eighteen.

Ethan - 12 years

Ethan Snowboarding

I haven't met Ethan yet.
He's been staying with his Mom in Atlanta.
I will meet him tonight.

I had a secret look around
Ethan's bedroom.

Messy!

Heavy metal music fan.

Videogame geek.

I don't think I want
a stepbrother!

I rub my knees and my elbow.
Then, I see the guy
watching me.
He's cute.
Oh no!

Did he see me try
that nose grind
on the rail?

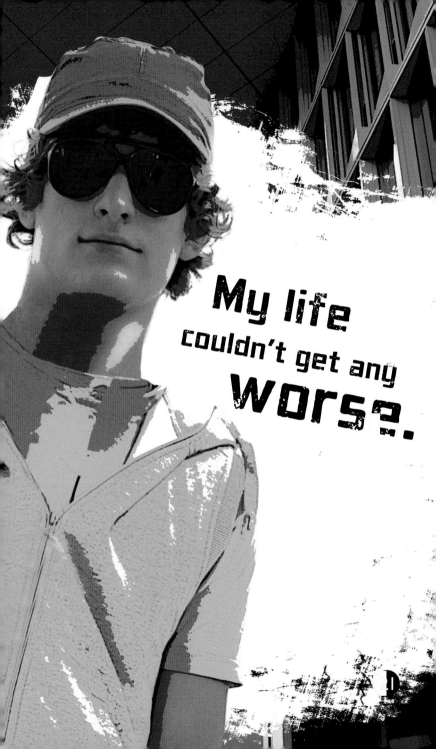

I stand up. I pick up my stuff.

My knees really hurt.

22

The cute guy is pulling my
deck from the tree.
He says, "You nearly did it."

I go bright red.
The guy saw me try that
nose grind on the rail.

"Try again," the guy says.
"Don't push down so hard
on the nose this time."

I look at the rail.
I think of the pain when
I hit the steps.
But I want to do it!
"OK," I say.

The guy hands me my deck.

He says,

"Go for it."

I walk up the steps.
The rail looks so high.
I've never pulled a nose
grind like this before.

The guy smiles at me,

**"You can
do it!"**

I push off.
I bend my knees.
I pull an ollie.

Yes! I'm on the rail.

My front truck is
grinding down the rail.

Focus

Stay cool

I remember—*Don't push down so hard on the nose.*

The grind is fast and smooth!

The rail ends.
I fly through the air
and land just right.

I did it!

The guy says, "Wow! I could never grind that rail."

He says, "You are really good."

I like this guy. I say, "Thanks, I did what you said. It worked!"

I say, "You must be a skater?"
He says, "Yes. I used to be."

I say, "I just moved here, but I hate it. There's no skate park."

The guy says, "There are places to skate. Come on, I'll show you."

We walk around
the town together.

He shows me some
great places to skate.

I like this guy.
I say, "I'm Taylor."
He smiles and says,
"I guessed."
I don't understand.
I say, "How did you guess?"

He says,
"I'm Ethan."

GRIND—WHAT'S NEXT?

A GRAFFITI TAG
ON YOUR OWN

Write your name in large pencil letters on a piece of paper.

- Draw an outline around each letter. Look at the tags on pages 40–41 for ideas.

- Use chalk to color the tag. Outline each letter in one color and color them in with another. Add highlights to your tag with white chalk.

- Spray hairspray over the tag to set it.

SKATER FILE
WITH A PARTNER

Find out more about skating using the Internet and books.

- Look up different stunts.
For example, ollie, grind, and kickflip.

- Look up different obstacles. For example, halfpipe, handrail, steps.

Make a SKATER FILE using your facts. Show what you have found out in words and pictures.

Imagine that Ethan and Taylor decide to campaign for a skate park. The city council asks them to present their case.

- Write down Taylor and Ethan's arguments for a skate park.
- Write down the city council's arguments against.
- Role-play the meeting. Did Taylor and Ethan win their campaign?

SKATE PARK
ON YOUR OWN / WITH A PARTNER / IN A GROUP

Imagine you have been asked to design a skate park.

- Think of a name for the park.
- What obstacles will it have?
- What else does the park have? For example, a café, a shop, restrooms, places to sit...
- Draw a plan of the skate park. Design a flyer to advertise it.

IF YOU ENJOYED THIS BOOK, TRY THESE OTHER **RiGHT NOW!** BOOKS.

It's just an old, empty house. Kristi must spend the night inside. Just Kristi and the ghost...

Tonight, Kayla must make a choice. Stay in Philadelphia with her boyfriend Ryan. Or start a new life in California.

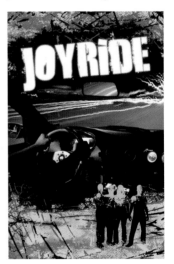

Tanner sees the red car. The keys are inside. Tanner says to Jacob, Bailey and Hannah, "Want to go for a drive?"

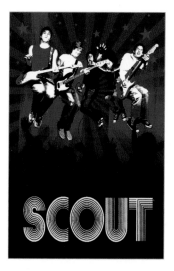

It's Saturday night.
Two angry guys. Two knives.
There's going to be a fight.

Tonight is the band's big
chance. Tonight, a record
company scout is at their gig!

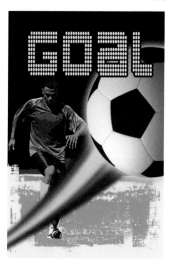

Damien's platoon is under
attack. Another soldier is in
danger. Damien must risk his
own life to save him.

Today is Carlos's tryout with
Chivas. There's just one place
up for grabs. But today,
everything is going wrong!

Suddenly we saw a missile. It was heading straight for us. A heat-seeking missile!

Alisha's online messages about Sam are getting nastier. Will anyone help Sam?

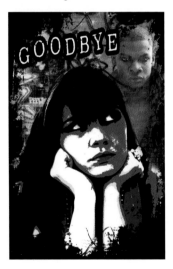

Laci and Jaden were in love, but then it all went wrong. Now Laci is with Joe. So why is Jaden always watching her?

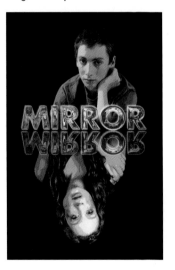

Will hates what he sees in the mirror. Brenna does too. Life would be so much better if only they looked different ...